Never Bet Your Best Friend!

"I'll bet you *anything* that all three of us make the soccer team," Missy proclaimed. She glanced at her friends, Emily and Willie. They gave her the thumbs-up sign.

"Anything?" asked Stephanie Cook.

"Anything," Missy repeated.

"How about your Old English sheepdog?"

Missy laughed out loud. She knew that Stephanie was only kidding around. "Sure! Sure! It's a bet!" Missy said. "But what do *I* get if *I* win the bet?"

"You'll get to see me lose," said Stephanie.

"What a bet!" Missy laughed. Then a chill ran down her back. Stephanie didn't *really* believe Missy had bet Baby—did she?

THE DREAM TEAM

by Molly Albright

illustrated by Dee deRosa

Troll Associates

Library of Congress Cataloging in Publication Data

Albright, Molly.
   The dream team.

   Summary: Missy, the class klutz, tries out for the
soccer team and receives some training tips from a
mysterious stranger.
   [1. Soccer—Fiction.   2. Mystery and detective stories]
I. deRosa, Dee, ill.   II. Title.
PZ7.A325Dr   1988   [Fic]   87-13821
ISBN 0-8167-1153-4 (lib. bdg.)
ISBN 0-8167-1154-2 (pbk.)

A TROLL BOOK, published by Troll Associates,
Mahwah, NJ 07430

THE DREAM TEAM

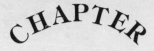

1

Melissa Fremont ran, huffing and puffing, down the soccer field. Somehow, she *had* to keep Stephanie Cook from getting past her and reaching the goal with the ball.

"Hey, Stephanie!" called Missy. "Did you know that the ancient Greeks blew up a cow's bladder and that was the first soccer ball?"

"That's gross," said Stephanie. "Why do you tell me things like that?"

"Because I hope it will slow you down," gasped Missy. Stephanie dribbled the ball expertly with her feet, keeping it clear of Missy.

"Hey, Stephanie! What newspaper does a cow read?" called Missy. Missy had found a joke book in the library recently. She had memorized an endless supply of riddles, jokes, and puns.

"I couldn't care less," replied Stephanie, not even sounding out of breath.

"*The Daily Moos*," Missy answered anyway.

"You're hopeless," said Stephanie. She held the ball between her feet and faked to the right. Missy shook back her mop of curly red hair. She stuck her tongue in the side of her mouth, trying to concentrate. She knew Stephanie was faking to the right, so Missy moved to the left.

But Stephanie double-faked. She went to the right after all. She dribbled the ball past Missy. Missy spun around, slipped on the wet grass, and landed on her bottom.

Stephanie paused for just a second and smiled. Then she kicked the ball between the goal posts.

A whistle blew. Missy and Stephanie walked to the sidelines.

"Good goal," admitted Missy.

"You gave me so much room," said Stephanie sweetly. "It was so easy to get past you."

Missy rolled her eyes. "So-o-o easy," she muttered.

Stephanie smiled. "I'm telling you only for your own good."

"All right! I want to see some hustle!" shouted Coach Harris.

Stephanie broke into a perky trot, running toward the coach.

Missy wanted to trip her. She was too tired to run another step. On days like this, Missy almost wished she had stayed home from school with Baby, her huge Old English sheepdog.

Baby was Missy's best friend. He was so enormous now, it was hard for Missy to remember that he had once been a tiny ball of fur. Missy had chosen him, just like her parents had chosen Missy, when she was a tiny baby waiting to be adopted.

It was Baby who had comforted Missy when the Fremonts first moved to Indianapolis from Cincinnati. Missy had gotten off to a bad start, trying to make friends in a new school. She'd even tried running away from home! But things had changed. Missy liked Hills Point School, and she had made some good friends. It was too bad Stephanie Cook was still such a pain. Missy was beginning to realize that some things *never* change!

As Missy slowly walked toward the coach, she noticed her teacher, Mrs. Kaufman, watching from the sidelines. Mrs. Kaufman had been Missy's teacher for only a few weeks, but she had quickly become Missy's all-time favorite.

"Missy, do you call that hustle?" shouted Coach Harris. "I want to see you move those feet."

Missy made it to the sideline and collapsed on the grass near Mrs. Kaufman. Standing next to Mrs. Kaufman was a woman Missy had never seen before. The woman stood up very straight and tall. Her black hair was cut in a short severe style, every hair perfectly in place.

"Who told you to sit down?" Stephanie hissed to Missy.

"My feet did," Missy replied. "They said, 'Missy, we can't hold you up anymore.' "

The woman with the short haircut looked at Missy and frowned. Missy blushed. She hadn't realized she had spoken so loudly.

"You'll have to talk to your feet, Missy," said Mrs. Kaufman. "Remember, better footwork, bigger feats."

Missy laughed. One of the things she loved about Mrs. Kaufman was her sense of humor. She always knew how to make Missy feel better. The other woman did not even crack a smile.

Mrs. Kaufman looked a little embarrassed.

"Coach Harris," said Stephanie. "Missy keeps trying to distract me with disgusting cow jokes."

"I was teaching her soccer history," protested Missy. "The first soccer ball was a cow's bladder."

"That happens to be true," said Coach Harris. "How did you know that, Missy?"

Missy shrugged. "I read it in a book."

Wilhelmina Wagnalls, Willie for short, the tallest girl in the class, stood up. "I refuse to kick around a cow's bladder."

Emily Green giggled. Emily had long dark hair and green eyes. She was built like a fireplug, short and stocky.

"That's enough, girls," said Coach Harris. "Remember, when I pick the varsity squad, I look for players who can become a team, not just individual stars. I'll be watching you during gym period in the next few weeks to see how you play together."

Missy plucked at a blade of grass. She didn't think she would make the team. She did not have the athletic talent to be a star. In fact, she was sort of a klutz. But Stephanie Cook definitely had star quality. Missy wondered if being a good team player meant going along with Stephanie all the time. She didn't think she could do that.

"Missy, when is a player offside?" Coach Harris asked. With a start, Missy realized she had not been listening as Coach Harris explained some more soccer rules.

"I—I don't know. . . ."

Coach Harris frowned. The woman standing next to Mrs. Kaufman frowned too. Her mouth formed into a grim straight line.

The coach continued his lesson, but Missy was still not paying attention. She watched the stern woman bend down and place her briefcase by her side. It looked like the kind of briefcase a spy might carry. In fact, Missy decided, the woman looked like a spy. She was wearing a belted trench coat with leather buttons and tall, shiny black leather boots.

"What's a spy doing on our soccer field?" Missy whispered to Stephanie, who was sitting next to her.

Stephanie stared at her. "What spy?"

Missy looked up. The mysterious woman was looking straight at her, and it was not a pleasant look. She looked as if she were trying to memorize Missy's features.

The woman whispered into Mrs. Kaufman's ear. Mrs. Kaufman listened respectfully and nodded her head. She looked flustered.

What if the woman spy were blackmailing Mrs. Kaufman? Maybe Missy would get a chance to save the lives of Mrs. Kaufman and her baby. Missy imagined the headlines: "Fearless girl nabs ferocious spy. A close call for Mrs. Kaufman and————" Missy couldn't fill in the end of the headline. That was because Mrs. Kaufman's baby hadn't been born yet. Missy didn't know the baby's name or whether it would be a boy or a girl. Anyway, Mrs. Kaufman would be grateful to Missy for the rest of her life. "Oh, Missy," she would cry. "I need you by my side forever."

Coach Harris blew his whistle again. Gym was over. "You'd better hustle and get back inside to change for your classes," he said. "I'm sorry I kept you a little late. There will be no time for showers."

Willie groaned. "I simply cannot go back to class smelling like a cow."

"Don't worry," said Stephanie. "Only little Miss Cow Bladder needs to clean up."

Missy stood up and brushed some grass from her legs. Her knees were covered with green stains. Stephanie's knees looked squeaky-clean.

Missy sighed as she left her daydream behind. All the daydreams in the world wouldn't help her make the varsity team. And she desperately wanted to do that. She was tired of being known as a klutz. If she really wanted to be in shape for soccer, she needed a plan.

CHAPTER

2

Slurp. Slurp.

Missy woke up with a start. Baby was giving her a wet wake-up kiss.

Missy looked at the digital clock by her bed. She threw off the covers. "No time for lying around," she said to Baby.

Baby jumped off the bed, his tongue hanging out. Missy hopped out after him. Her purple sweat shirt and silver running shorts were on the chair by her bed. She had carefully put them there the night before. She'd picked out a purple bandanna for Baby too.

Missy dressed quickly and ran downstairs. She needed lots of room for her warm-ups. She pushed aside the leather easy chair and footstool.

Then she flattened her mother's exercise book on the floor so she could read it. *Steely Stomachs in Twenty Days.* Perfect. The tryouts for the soccer team were in exactly three weeks, and Missy would be ready! Mrs. Kaufman would be so impressed.

Missy studied the diagrams at the beginning of the book. "Why bother with the sissy stuff?" she thought. She would skip straight to the "superathlete" sit ups. After all, that was her goal—to be a superathlete instead of a klutz.

"Have a friend hold your feet or hook them under a couch," Missy read from the book.

She looked at Baby. She put out her feet. "Sit," she commanded.

Baby sat on Missy's ankles.

Missy glanced at the book by her side. "Touch your elbows to your knees," she read.

When Missy tried to touch her elbow to her knee, Baby jumped up. Missy landed on her back with a thud.

Missy took a deep breath. "You're no help," she said. "Go lie down." She gave Baby a cloth bunny, one of his favorite toys. Baby lay down with the bunny between his paws and stared at her.

Missy frowned. Her feet wouldn't fit under the couch. She looked around the living room.

The coffee table was perfect. She pulled it away from the couch. Then she lay down with her feet hooked under the lower shelf of the table and rolled up, touching her elbow to her knee. She did five quick sit ups in a row, and then she couldn't breathe.

She lay on the floor, huffing and puffing.

"This is not fun," Missy muttered to herself.

But Baby thought it looked like fun. Halfway through her next sit up, he pounced on Missy. She gave a shriek, and her feet flew into the air, tipping over the coffee table. Everything on the table went flying—newspapers, books, her father's sheet music for his viola, Missy's homework, and a half-eaten cookie.

Missy's father came bounding down the stairs.

"Dad," exclaimed Missy. "What are you doing?"

Mr. Fremont stopped and stared at the mess. "What's going on? Are you all right?"

"I'm getting in shape, Dad," said Missy with all the dignity she could muster.

Mr. Fremont watched Baby eat the rest of the cookie. "I knew I left that down here when I was practicing," he said. Mr. Fremont played first viola with the Indianapolis Symphony.

He helped Missy set the coffee table in front of the couch, and together they cleaned up the mess.

"What's this new shape-up program?" Mr. Fremont asked Missy.

"I have a plan," she replied. "I'm going to try to make the varsity soccer team."

Missy watched her father's face carefully. Mr. Fremont knew what a truly terrible athlete Missy was. He yawned. "What about swimming?"

"You know my school doesn't have a pool. Besides, what's so great about swimming?"

"You can do it lying down."

Missy groaned. "Time for my run," she said.

She picked up Baby's leash. Baby was so excited about going out that he wagged his tail against the pile of papers on the coffee table, sending them flying to the floor again.

Mr. Fremont sighed. "I guess you and Baby are just two of a kind."

Missy grinned and ran out the door.

The air was damp, the sky was gray, and it looked as if it were going to pour. "Real winners don't let a little rain stop them," Missy said to Baby. He looked as though he didn't want to leave the front porch. Baby hated the rain.

Missy ran down the block. Baby followed her unhappily. But when he saw another dog, he perked up, bounding through the wet leaves.

"Baby!" shouted Missy. The other dog cowered between the legs of its owner, who was covered from head to foot by a bright pink rain slicker.

Baby skidded to a stop in front of the dog.

"He won't hurt your dog," called Missy. She knew that some people were afraid of big dogs.

"*I* know that," said a voice from within the slicker. "But you won't be able to convince my dog."

Mrs. Kaufman poked her face out of the hood.

"I didn't know you had a dog," exclaimed Missy, surprised and pleased at this chance meeting with her teacher. She caught Baby by the collar and pulled him away from Mrs. Kaufman's dog,

who was shivering with fear. The dog was a mutt, with a large terrier's head and floppy ears, a long hairy body and short stumpy legs.

"I just got her," said Mrs. Kaufman. "She was a stray. Her name is Cleo. Silly-looking, isn't she?"

Missy agreed, but she didn't want to say so. "Maybe she'll grow."

"The vet thinks she's already five or six years old."

Baby wagged his tail and looked so friendly that finally Cleo took a step forward and wagged her own tail.

"This is the first time I've seen Cleo so interested in another dog," said Mrs. Kaufman. "I found her on the street. I have a feeling her owners abandoned her a long time ago. I hate people who do that. She's afraid of almost everything—big dogs, rainy days, being alone. In fact, she's just a big baby herself."

"Baby hates the rain too. Maybe you should hire Baby and me to baby-sit."

Mrs. Kaufman laughed. "For Cleo or for this new baby?" she asked, patting her stomach.

Missy knew that Mrs. Kaufman would soon be leaving school to have her baby. She also knew that she'd miss her favorite teacher—a lot!

Mrs. Kaufman looked at her watch. "I'd better be going, or we'll both be late for school."

"Oh, no!" cried Missy. "I haven't even run a mile. Day one and I'm already behind."

"Day one of what?" asked Mrs. Kaufman.

"Missy Fremont's shape-up plan. I'm going to work hard to make the varsity soccer team."

Mrs. Kaufman gave Missy a strange look. Missy hoped it wasn't pity. Maybe she should have kept her plan a secret.

Missy turned to leave and tripped over her shoelace, staggering forward. "I guess I'm not off to a very good start," she said. " 'Bye, Mrs. Kaufman! See you in class."

Missy held on to Baby's collar as they ran. "Mrs. Kaufman's the greatest," she said to Baby.

Baby nodded his head.

Mrs. Fremont was up and dressed by the time Missy returned. She was sitting in the kitchen, eating a piece of coffee cake and reading a book called *Flatter Fannies*. Mr. Fremont had left to go to an early rehearsal.

"Dad told me about your new shape-up plan," Mrs. Fremont said.

Missy sighed. "I want to make the soccer team more than anything, Mom. I'm sick of being a klutz. I figure the soccer team will give me a whole new image."

"You certainly gave our living room a new image," said Mrs. Fremont, pouring Missy a glass of milk.

Missy laughed. "I ran into Mrs. Kaufman," she said. "She was out walking her new dog."

"Hmm," said Mrs. Fremont. "I wonder when exactly she'll be leaving school." Mrs. Fremont was also a teacher. She was substituting for several weeks in a kindergarten class not far from Missy's school.

"I think she said her baby was due next month," said Missy. "I hope she stays until the very last minute."

"I really doubt that she will," her mother replied.

"Boy, do I have bad luck!" Missy groaned. "She's the best teacher I've ever known."

Missy buttered a piece of toast. "She should have planned better and had a baby in the summer—or next year, when I wouldn't be her student."

"Missy, you know those things can't always be planned."

"You planned when you adopted me," said Missy angrily. "And *I* planned when I adopted Baby. It's not fair. I hate babies."

Baby heard his name and sat up. He looked at Missy with a worried expression.

Missy shook her head. "Well, maybe not *all* babies. Not you."

"Maybe you're worrying for nothing," said Mrs. Fremont. "I'm sure that whoever replaces Mrs. Kaufman will be just as nice."

"No way," Missy thought.

She ran upstairs, showered, and changed into her school clothes. Then she grabbed her knapsack. Perhaps Mrs. Kaufman would stay to the very end. "Maybe by the time she leaves," Missy said to her mother as she hurried out the door, "I'll have made the soccer team. Maybe I'll even be captain, and Mrs. Kaufman will be at our first game, cheering for me all the way. And you and Dad too," Missy added quickly.

"Don't forget Baby," said Mrs. Fremont. "Baby would make a wonderful cheerleader."

"Right. We can tie pompoms around his neck."

Baby put his head between his paws. He looked as if the very idea of pompoms was completely undignified.

CHAPTER 3

Stephanie Cook was standing outside Missy's house, looking annoyed. Stephanie lived on the same block as Missy, and considered it a great favor that she allowed Missy to wait with her for the school bus.

"Sorry, I'm late," said Missy, carrying another piece of toast with her. She hadn't had time to finish her breakfast. "But guess what! I ran into Mrs. Kaufman this morning. She has the most adorable new dog—"

"Cleo," interrupted Stephanie. "Short for Cleopatra, the Queen of the Nile. I've seen her. I think mixed breeds have so much more character than purebreds, don't you?"

"Baby is a purebred English sheepdog, and I think he's got plenty of character," said Missy.

"Oh, I'm sorry," said Stephanie. "I didn't mean to insult your big Baby."

Missy rolled her eyes. Only Stephanie could make Missy feel bad that Baby *wasn't* a mutt.

When the bus arrived, Missy and Stephanie walked to the rear, where Emily and Wilhelmina were sitting. Emily stared at Missy's toast, which was dripping with butter.

"How can you eat that in front of me?" she asked. "All I have to do is look at food and I gain weight."

"The problem is that you *eat* while you're looking," Stephanie pointed out. "If only you would *look* and not *eat*."

Missy broke off half a piece of toast and gave it to Emily.

Stephanie sighed. "A true friend would support Emily's attempts to get her weight under control."

"You make her sound like a blimp," said Missy. "Emily, you're not fat, just plump."

"Hey, Emily," Missy continued. "I'm exercising so I can make the varsity soccer team. Mom has all these shape-up books. How would you like to exercise with me? It would be much more fun with a buddy."

Emily looked with envy at Missy's slim figure. "I don't get it, why do *you* have to get in shape?"

"Oh, she's in shape all right," said Stephanie with a giggle. "But you obviously haven't watched her playing soccer. Missy is the original Miss Klutz."

Missy ignored Stephanie. "Soccer is going to be my sport. I'm working out every day. I'll be ready."

"Sure, if you get two new feet," Stephanie snickered.

"Lay off her, Steph," said Emily. "You never know, maybe Missy will turn out to be the greatest soccer player of all time."

"Forget it. You need good rhythm and coordination to play soccer. In fact, it's important in all sports," answered Stephanie.

"Then I'm sunk," said Missy. Missy couldn't keep a beat if her life depended on it. Even when she listened to rock music she always clapped at the wrong times.

"Maybe I'll try out for the soccer team too," said Willie.

"You?" Stephanie exclaimed.

Willie often said that her favorite sport was lying on the couch and watching TV. She didn't know anything about baseball, basketball, or hockey. And although she was tall, slim, and looked like a ballerina, Wilhelmina had all the grace of a giraffe on roller skates.

"I have long legs," said Willie. "I think I would look good in shorts and those striped shirts."

"Great!" said Missy. "We can start our own club."

"How adorable," said Stephanie. "You can call it the Klutz Klub."

"I wish we were playing that game that has a puck. 'Puck' sounds so cute," said Willie.

"That's hockey," Missy told her.

"As long as I don't have to wear those silly shoulder pads," said Wilhelmina.

"Don't worry," said Missy. "You don't have to wear shoulder pads."

"Oh, good."

"This is going to be some club," said Stephanie.

"You can join," said Missy. "We don't want to leave anybody out."

"You must be joking. Besides, the coach already asked me to try out."

"Then you won't mind if Willie and I work out with Missy," said Emily. "You already *know* you're going to make the team."

"Of course I don't mind," Stephanie said haughtily, pretending not to care. "I think it's charming that Wilhelmina has finally taken an interest in sports, and I think it's wonderful that *you,* Emily, are on your ten-thousandth plan to lose weight. I wish you all the luck in the world."

"Thanks a *lot,*" said Emily.

"I'll bet you *anything* that all three of us make the team," Missy proclaimed.

"Anything?" asked Stephanie.

"Anything," repeated Missy.

"How about your purebred English sheepdog?"

Missy laughed. She knew Stephanie was just kidding around. After all, she didn't even *like* purebreds. Hadn't she said so earlier? Missy decided to go along with the joke. "Sure! Sure!" she laughed. "It's a bet!"

Stephanie nodded and settled back in her seat.

"You know, I think it's charming that the three of you are going to help one another out," she said sweetly.

Missy giggled.

"What do *I* get when we make the team and *you* lose the bet?" she asked.

"You'll get to see me lose," said Stephanie. "Won't that be enough?"

"You bet!"

Missy laughed. Stephanie didn't.

As the bus pulled up in front of the school, Missy watched Stephanie get up to leave. She looked smug.

A chill ran down Missy's back. Stephanie didn't *really* believe Missy had bet Baby—did she?

When Missy and her classmates entered their room, Mrs. Kaufman was not at her desk. The first period of the day was reserved for creative writing, and it was Missy's favorite part of school. Missy loved to write for Mrs. Kaufman because Mrs. Kaufman loved what Missy wrote.

Missy waited impatiently. She doodled in her notebook. At last Mrs. Kaufman walked into the classroom. She was followed by that strange woman who looked like a spy. The woman was wearing black pants and a black sweater with a high turtleneck. Mrs. Kaufman was dressed in a pale blue maternity dress. Her light brown hair hung in soft curls around her head.

"Good morning, class," said Mrs. Kaufman. "May I have your attention."

Mrs. Kaufman sounded very formal. Missy stopped doodling and looked up.

Mrs. Kaufman cleared her throat. "I have an announcement that is both good news and bad news. The bad news is that I will be leaving school sooner than I expected. As you know, I am having a baby in just a few weeks. I was going to stay on longer, but I've decided that I really need some time to prepare for the new baby. This, class, is Ms. Van Sickel. She will be substituting for me while I'm out. That's the good news." Mrs. Kaufman looked around at all the sad faces and added, "And I think we're very lucky to have her with us."

Missy slumped in her chair. "That's the most sickening good news I've ever heard," she whispered to Stephanie, who sat next to her.

Stephanie sat straight at her desk with her hands neatly folded.

Missy raised her hand. "Can't you stay for just a little while longer?"

Mrs. Kaufman shook her head. "I'm sorry, Missy. Ms. Van Sickel, this is Missy Fremont."

"I prefer to meet the students in alphabetical order," said Ms. Van Sickel. She put her briefcase on the desk with a clunk. There was no question about who was in charge of the class now.

Mrs. Kaufman read from the class list, and each student stood up. Ms. Van Sickel gave each of them a piercing stare. By the time the introductions were finished, the first period was over.

Mrs. Kaufman stood in front of the class. "It was quite a stroke of luck for me that Ms. Van Sickel was available today, because I have a doctor's appointment. I was going to arrange for a substitute this morning. Now this will give you a chance to get to know one another."

Mrs. Kaufman smiled at Ms. Van Sickel, who didn't return her smile. Then Mrs. Kaufman left the classroom. Missy wished she could go with her. She felt as if her class were being left alone with a witch for a teacher.

Ms. Van Sickel rapped her knuckles on the desk. "In order to get to know you, I will administer a series of tests today. I want no talking while the papers are handed out. Wilhelmina Wagnalls, will you please step forward."

Willie stood up. She was nearly as tall as Ms. Van Sickel herself.

"I have rules in my classroom," said Ms. Van Sickel. "Whenever papers or books are passed out, there must be absolute silence. Too often children think this is a time to whisper and gossip. I will have none of that."

Willie looked frightened as she took the test papers and started to hand them out. When she reached Missy's desk, she tripped over Missy's knapsack, which was in the aisle. The papers went flying out of her hand.

Missy stood up to help Willie, and she and Willie collided. Missy's chair crashed to the floor.

The class began to snicker. Willie turned beet-red.

"What's going on?" demanded Ms. Van Sickel.

"Just a little accident," said Missy. She bent down to pick up her test paper, but it was stuck under the leg of her desk, and she ripped it.

She showed the two halves to Ms. Van Sickel. "May I have another one?" she asked.

"There is only one to a customer," Ms. Van Sickel said. Then she turned to Willie. "Wilhelmina, you are like a bull in a china shop."

Missy thought she was going to explode. She didn't like Ms. Van Sickel picking on Willie. But she kept her mouth shut.

Missy walked slowly down the aisle to her desk.

"Miss Fremont, please take your seat. Try to put the two halves of your test paper together and settle down. This is a classroom, not the slapstick comedy hour."

The words on the ripped paper swam in front of Missy's eyes. She was so angry and embarrassed. Mrs. Kaufman would have understood.

But now Mrs. Kaufman was gone. In her place was Ms. *Van Sickening*, who had no understanding at all.

Missy could hardly answer the questions. It was all she could do not to cry.

CHAPTER 4

"I've never had a more rotten week in my life," Missy announced on Saturday.

Her mother looked sympathetic. "It'll get better."

Missy tied the shoelaces on her sneakers into a double bow. "I don't think so, Mom. It will probably get worse. Ms. Van Sickel gave us back our tests. I got an *F*. I'll probably flunk out of school."

"Missy, put that F behind you. You're a very good student. You just got off on the wrong foot. Think about *good* things, like the way you and Emily and Wilhelmina are helping one another make the team."

"Helping, ha!" exploded Missy. "Yesterday Emily ran a mile in exactly seventeen minutes and fifty-five seconds. Most people *walk* faster than that. Willie got a blister because she insisted on wearing glitter socks instead of sweat socks. Some great team!" Missy shuddered at the next thought. "And if we lose, there goes Baby—maybe!" she muttered.

"What?"

"Uh, nothing. It's just an expression."

"It's not one I've ever heard."

Missy hadn't mentioned her so-called bet with Stephanie. Her mother had always warned her against making stupid bets.

And if Stephanie believed she had an actual bet with Missy, then the bet was *very* stupid. Missy stood to lose far more than she could possibly gain. However, Missy was still pretty sure Stephanie had been kidding. She was also sure that if the worst happened and she lost, Stephanie wouldn't *really* ask for Baby. Even Stephanie Cook couldn't separate Missy from her best friend, Baby.

Mrs. Fremont looked puzzled. "I'm sorry you've gotten off to such a bad start with your new teacher. Usually you do so well in school."

"There's nothing *usual* about Ms. Van Sickening."

"Missy, you'd better stop calling her that. One day you'll forget who you're talking to, and you'll say it to her face. You don't need that."

"She can't hate me any more than she already does."

The doorbell rang. "I'll get it," said Missy.

Baby followed Missy to the door. It was the

mail carrier. "I've got a package for Missy Fremont," she said. "It wouldn't fit into your mailbox."

"A package for me?" asked Missy. "It's not my birthday. I never get packages except at Christmas and my birthday."

"Are you Missy Fremont?"

Missy nodded.

"Then you should never say 'never.' Sign here, please."

Missy signed for her package. She turned it over. There was no return address, just her name written in block letters.

"Who's that for?" asked her mother when Missy returned to the kitchen.

"It's for me," said Missy, handing Mrs. Fremont the rest of the mail. "And it's not from Grandma. It's got an Indianapolis postmark."

"Well, stop being a detective and open it."

Missy tore open the brown wrapper. She held up a book, *All About Soccer,* by Jared Lebow.

"Mom, thanks," said Missy. "It's got to be more help than *Steely Stomachs.*"

"I didn't send you that," said Mrs. Fremont.

"Did Dad?"

"You can ask him," said Mrs. Fremont. "But he didn't mention it."

Missy went down to the basement, where her father was practicing the viola. She waited until he paused. Then she showed him the book.

"I didn't send it," said Mr. Fremont.

Missy studied her father's face. She knew he

could tease her sometimes, but he didn't have that funny look in his eye. She believed him. He hadn't sent her the book. But who had?

Missy put the book into her knapsack and took it to the park, where she was meeting Willie and Emily. When they reached the park, she let Baby off his leash, and he bounded after a pigeon.

Missy showed Emily and Wilhelmina the book as soon as they arrived. Neither of them knew who could have sent it.

"Maybe we have a secret admirer," said Wilhelmina. "I've always felt I was destined to have secret admirers."

"Who would ever imagine that the way to Willie's heart was a book on *soccer*," Emily said.

"Well, anyway, we can use all the coaching we can get," said Missy. "Even from a secret coach." She sat cross-legged on the ground, opened the book, and studied the diagrams for different kicks. "Look at this," she said, pointing to something called the banana kick.

She read aloud from the book. "The banana kick is one of the most difficult to master. It is particularly effective on corner kicks because the ball swerves to confuse the goaltender and draw him out of position."

Baby came back, and Missy patted him absent-mindedly. Then she stood up and continued reading: "To swerve the ball from left to right, the kicker must make contact with the right side of the ball, using part of his instep and part of his toes, almost wrapping the front part of the foot around the ball."

Emily frowned. "It sounds awfully confusing. But I *love* bananas."

"Give me the ball," said Missy. She walked backward almost fifty feet and then ran full tilt toward the ball. She tried to wrap the front part of her foot around the ball, but she overstepped and tripped, falling flat on her face.

Baby ran to Missy and licked her. "I'm all right," said Missy, patting Baby on the neck. Then she noticed something tucked under Baby's collar. It was a piece of yellow paper.

Carefully, Missy pulled it out. "Try the banana kick from just a few steps away. Don't take a running lead," the note read.

Missy's mouth dropped open. "Emily! Willie! Come here!" She showed them the note. "Did you write this?"

Emily and Willie looked at each other. "We were watching you," said Emily. "Neither of us wrote anything."

Missy, Emily, and Willie looked around. The park seemed completely deserted.

"Where did you get the note?" Emily asked.

"It was stuck under Baby's collar," Missy replied. "Baby, where did you get this?"

Baby wagged his tail.

"This is spooky," said Emily.

"Yoo-hoo!" called Missy. "Whoever is out there, will you please show yourself!"

The girls couldn't see anything except some leaves rustling in the wind.

"I think it's romantic," said Willie with a sigh.

"What's romantic about telling someone how to do a banana kick?" asked Missy, but she did think it was exciting that someone wanted to give them this special secret help.

"Okay, let's see if this advice really works," Emily suggested. She placed the ball on the grass.

Missy backed up just a few feet. She moved toward the ball, twisting her foot. The ball sailed in an arc, flying in a curve that would have impressed even Stephanie.

Missy clapped her hands. "All right!" she cried. Missy had always kicked the ball as hard as she could. But she hadn't realized there were things you could do to control it.

"That's terrific!" shouted Emily. "The banana kick will be our secret weapon."

Missy grinned. "What did the boy banana say to the girl banana?"

"You have a lot of appeal," answered Emily, who had borrowed Missy's joke book. "Why don't bananas get lonely?" she asked, giggling.

"Because they go around in bunches," shouted Missy.

"I have one," said Wilhelmina. "What did the banana do when the monkey chased it?"

"The banana split," cried Emily and Missy. They were laughing so hard they could barely talk.

"We're going to kill them with bad jokes," said

Wilhelmina, lying on the ground, gasping for air.

"Maybe our secret friend can send us some bad riddles," said Missy.

Emily wasn't finished yet.

"What's the easiest way to make a banana split?" she asked.

"Tell it to get out of town," replied Willie, proud that she knew one of the answers.

"I've got one," said Missy. "This is my father's favorite. Why is a banana peel on the sidewalk like music?"

Both Emily and Wilhelmina looked blank.

"Because if you don't C sharp, you'll B flat," said Missy. They all laughed until it hurt.

"Okay, everybody! We'd better get back to our practicing," Missy said finally. "We may have a secret coach, but we still have a lot of work to do!"

CHAPTER

5

Having a secret friend even made going back to school and facing Ms. Van Sickel seem all right. But who was the secret coach? Missy was determined to find out. That was work for a real detective, and Missy liked mysteries. She wondered if she should wear a disguise. On Monday morning Missy came down to the breakfast table, whistling.

"Dad, do you think I'd look good in a mustache?" she asked.

"I see you more in sideburns and a beard," answered her father. "Why?"

"I was thinking of going to school in a disguise."

"Are things that bad with Ms. Van Sickel?"

"Actually yes. But I wasn't thinking of her. I'm going to be a detective today. I want to find out who sent me that book and the note.

It's a real mystery. Do you *promise* it wasn't you?"

"It wasn't either of us," replied Mrs. Fremont.

Missy believed her. Her parents wouldn't lie to her. But who could it be? Not that many people knew how important it was for Missy to make the team. Even fewer knew of her ridiculous bet with Stephanie.

"Maybe your mother and I should meet with Ms. Van Sickel," said Mr. Fremont. "We don't like to see you unhappy with school. You've always loved it."

Missy didn't want her parents to talk to Ms. Van Sickel. "Thanks, Dad, but I can handle it. You can talk to her soon enough at the parent-teacher conferences."

"Actually, we'll meet her sooner than that," said Mrs. Fremont. "I want to invite her to the shower I'm giving for Mrs. Kaufman. Mrs. Kaufman herself put Ms. Van Sickel on the guest list."

"You're giving a shower for Mrs. Kaufman?" exclaimed Missy. "Why didn't you tell me?"

"I *am* telling you. We just decided on it yesterday. A group of teachers in the district wanted to have one, and I offered to have it here. I thought you'd be thrilled."

"Mom, I just wish you'd have asked me."

"I didn't realize it would upset you."

"Upset me! Having Ms. Van Sickening in our *house*? You might as well invite Frankenstein."

"Missy, watch your tone of voice," warned her

mother. "You were practicing all day yesterday. This is the first opportunity I've had to talk to you about it. In fact, Mrs. Kaufman thought it would be nice if you and some of your classmates were invited to the shower too. She's very fond of you, you know."

Missy took a deep breath. "I know. I'm sorry."

Missy looked at her mom and thought a bit. "Did you mean that you and I would give the party *together*?" she asked.

"That's what I had in mind before you snapped my head off."

"I'm sorry, Mom. It's really a great idea. We can invite Emily and Willie. And Stephanie too. Then we can show Stephanie *and* Ms. Van Sickel what spectacular parties we put on. Stephanie is always so perfect. Now's our chance to be perfect too."

Mrs. Fremont smiled. "Well, I don't know about perfect, but we could throw a great party together."

Missy grinned. "Dad and I can make our special chocolate-chocolate cake. Mrs. Kaufman loves chocolate. Mom, this is a great idea! I'm glad we thought of it."

"We?" Mrs. Fremont smiled.

"Maybe even Ms. Van Sickel will like Dad's chocolate-chocolate cake. Although knowing her, she's probably allergic to chocolate. She's allergic to *anything* that's good."

"Missy," warned her mother.

"Okay, no more Van Sickening jokes. When will we have the party?"

"Mrs. Kaufman said that a week from Saturday would be good."

"That's right before the tryouts. They're on Monday."

"That'll be good," said Mr. Fremont. "You should taper off your training. And the party will take your mind off soccer."

Missy nodded thoughtfully. "Who knows? Maybe the party will bring me good luck. I sure can use all the luck I can get."

Mr. Fremont was puzzled. "I know you want to make the team, Missy, but the world won't end if you don't."

Missy looked down at Baby, who was sleeping at her feet. "But if Stephanie is taking this bet seriously, it could be the end of the world as we know it," she said softly.

Later, on the bus, Missy tried to avoid any mention of soccer or her bet with Stephanie, but it was no use.

"Hey, Stephanie," said Willie. "You'd better get ready for us on the soccer field. Missy has discovered a secret weapon."

Stephanie arched one eyebrow, a trick Missy wished she could do. "A secret weapon?"

Missy tried to change the subject. "Hey, guess what, you guys. My mother and I are giving a shower for Mrs. Kaufman. It's going to be for teachers and parents and kids. You three are the first people I'm inviting."

"What a neat idea," said Willie.

Stephanie looked torn between wanting to refuse and not wanting to be left out. She hated to be left out of things.

"Maybe we can make banana-kick bread," joked Emily.

"What are you talking about?" demanded Stephanie.

"Oh, just a little soccer kick Missy's learning."

"See if you can get this one," Missy said quickly. "What did the boy banana say to the girl banana?"

"Who cares?" said Stephanie.

"I know," Emily giggled. " 'You have a lot of appeal'!"

"That is the stupidest joke I've ever heard," replied Stephanie. "Honestly, Emily, I think all that exercise has turned your brain to mush. You're acting like a baby." Stephanie's face was pale except for two red dots on her cheeks.

She glared at Missy. "Well, Miss Banana Kick, you'd better make a list of the things your big Baby likes to eat. And I'd better stock up on dog food."

"Hey, Stephanie," said Emily. "You know that bet was just a joke. You can't take Missy's dog away from her."

Stephanie scowled. "Baby is a pathetic name for such a beautiful dog," she said.

"Pathetic!" cried Missy. "Who are you calling pathetic?"

Stephanie smiled, happy to have made Missy really angry. "I think it's pathetic to give a dog a 'baby' name. Only a baby would do that."

Missy was so angry she could hardly speak. She hadn't been a baby when she named Baby. She'd been seven years old.

Actually, Missy had hesitated before giving Baby his name. She'd been worried that she would be teased just the way Stephanie was teasing her now. But her parents had told her that she shouldn't worry about what anybody else said. If she wanted to call her dog Baby, then Baby would be his name.

"*I'll* call him Lord Stephan," said Stephanie with a fake English accent, "since my name is the female version of Stephan. That way everyone will know he belongs to me."

"You're not going to be calling him anything," said Missy. "Besides, Lord Stephan is a dumb name for a dog."

"I think it's elegant," said Stephanie haughtily. "Like me."

Missy made gagging noises with her hands on her throat. Stephanie glared at her.

"Don't let her get to you," said Emily.

Missy sighed. "That's easier said than done. What if she really makes me stick to the dumb bet? I was just joking, you know. And I thought she was too."

Emily winked at her. "You're forgetting something—we *could* all make the team. Then *you'd* win the bet!"

Missy looked down at the green soccer book,

lying on top of her notebook. "You're right," she said. "Maybe our secret coach has secret powers we don't know about."

"What are you talking about?" asked Stephanie suspiciously.

"You'll see," said Missy.

CHAPTER
6

On Friday Missy showed up for soccer practice early. She changed in the locker room, and then brought the large green soccer book out to the field. She put it on the bench. She wanted to see who noticed it.

Coach Harris looked at the book. "I see you're doing more research," he said.

Missy looked up at him. Could *he* be her secret friend? Did Coach Harris secretly want Missy to make the team?

Coach Harris picked up the book and leafed through it. "I don't think you can learn sports from a book," he said. "Basics. That's what's important. I'd much rather have you out there practicing skills like dribbling or learning how to head the ball. In soccer, a hard head is better than a head crammed with facts." He laughed.

"I know that, but a book can help, don't you think?" Missy asked.

Coach Harris put the book down. "No book can teach you what *I* can teach you. Besides, I've seen that Jared Lebow on television. He's a smart guy, but he's never played soccer. He just writes about it because he loves the sport."

Missy thought that was probably a good reason to write about something. However, she crossed Coach Harris off her list of people who might be her secret coach.

Missy laced up her shoes and ran onto the field. She began to dribble the ball around, waiting for the other kids to join her.

On the sidelines she saw a familiar, slightly bulging outline. By its side was a long hairy dog with short legs. Mrs. Kaufman was talking to a group of mothers who had come to watch soccer practice. Ms. Van Sickel was there, too, standing alone.

Coach Harris blew his whistle. He sent students up and down the field doing wind sprints. Missy discovered that her shape-up plan had helped. She was much less out of breath than she had been just two weeks ago. Willie and Emily were able to keep up with her too.

"All right," shouted Coach Harris. "I want to do some one-on-one drills. Wilhelmina, I'm going to try you as goalie. You've got the wing-spread for it."

Willie stood with her hands on her hips. "Wing-spread? You make me sound like a vulture."

"Think of yourself as a mother eagle," said Coach Harris. "I want you to guard your nest, okay? So, into the cage. Missy, I want you to go one-on-one with Stephanie defending. Stephanie, if you get the ball away from Missy, turn into an attacker, and head for the goal. Willie, your job is to stop them both."

Willie trotted past Missy. "Remember the old banana kick," she whispered into Missy's ear. "I want you to make a monkey out of her."

Missy swallowed.

Stephanie stood opposite Missy. "Come on," she said. "Let's get this over with."

Missy dribbled the ball, hoping that her new speed would allow her to get around Stephanie. But Stephanie rushed forward, placing herself squarely in front of Missy.

Missy nudged the ball with her instep and galloped after it, but the ball went too far. Stephanie trapped it with her knee, stopped it, and moved her head to the left. Missy fell for the fake, and Stephanie triumphantly dribbled the ball right by her. Missy went after her, furious as a bull. She shouldered Stephanie, trying to force her to give up the ball.

The coach ran beside them. "That's the spirit," he yelled. But Stephanie was too fast for Missy. She swept around her and kicked the ball far down the field.

Willie came out toward the penalty line to meet her. "Remember, Wilhelmina," called the coach, "keep your body between the goal and the ball."

Stephanie stepped up the pace. She booted the ball hard and squarely, but Willie was right there to stop it from going in. She caught it and fell backward.

"Great save!" shouted Coach Harris.

He looked back at Missy. "Take a rest. I'll give you another chance in a few minutes. Next two."

Missy flopped down on the sidelines. She had been totally outclassed by Stephanie. Even Willie had shown her up. Next thing she would know, Willie would make the team, and Missy would be left out.

Missy pulled herself together and went to the bench, where the coach kept a cooler of water. She picked up a paper cup. Then she stopped and stared. At the bottom of the cup was a small square of yellow paper.

Missy pulled it out and unfolded it. "When you dribble, take short choppy steps and just nudge the ball."

Missy looked around. Nobody was near the bench. She studied the handwriting. It looked a little familiar, but she couldn't place it.

She picked up the cooler to get her drink. On the bottom of the cooler she felt something flap in the breeze. It was another yellow note! This one read, "Watch her hips, not her head. Her hips will tell you in which direction she's going."

Missy studied the note. "Hips, not head," she muttered to herself.

"Did you see me out there?" asked Emily. "I

was great. I made my opponent give up the ball, and I saved a goal."

"I missed it," said Missy. "I got two more notes from our secret coach. Whoever it is, he sure knows a lot about soccer."

"Well, you can rule out my mom," said Emily. "She's over there talking to Mrs. Kaufman. She asked me why I didn't use my *hands* more! She doesn't even know that's against the rules."

"What about Willie's mom? Could she be our secret friend?"

"I don't think so. She's a model. She's been away all week at a fashion show."

"Well, it's got to be somebody around here," said Missy.

Just then the coach blew his whistle. "Fremont and Cook, I want you again."

Missy ran to midfield, practicing her short half-steps.

"What are you doing?" asked Stephanie, frowning.

"Never mind," said Missy.

Stephanie shrugged. "You can start with the ball," she said with a smile. "Taking it away from you is like taking candy from a *Baby*."

Missy licked her lips.

"Okay, you two," said Coach Harris. "Stephanie, why are you defending again?"

"It's my choice. I want to give Missy another chance."

Missy dribbled the ball toward Stephanie. Stephanie charged, but Missy kicked the ball to the right, just a bit. Stephanie moved toward it, but Missy juggled it past her to the right again, taking quick, small steps, keeping the ball just inches from her instep.

Stephanie's eyes locked onto Missy's. Missy turned to fake to the right again, but Stephanie was with her.

Stephanie glanced at the coach. He was setting up the next group. She stuck out her foot and deliberately tripped Missy.

Missy crashed to the ground.

Stephanie stole the ball and dribbled down the field. Missy jumped up and ran after her. She caught up with Stephanie and moved between her and the goal.

Stephanie slowed down her dribbling to control the ball. She moved her head to the left. Missy didn't fall for the fake. She was staring at Stephanie's hips, and they had pivoted to the right. When Stephanic tried to pass to the right, Missy was there to intercept the ball.

She touched it with the outside of her right foot, putting it out of Stephanie's reach. Then she pulled up close to the goal.

Willie came out, ready for her. Missy could hear Stephanie panting behind her. She knew that in a split second Stephanie would catch up to her. And she knew Stephanie would do anything to stop her. Missy didn't hesitate.

She planted her left foot next to the ball. She

bent back her right leg and brought her instep solidly against the center of the ball, curving it just slightly.

Missy watched the ball take off, low and straight. Willie lunged at it, but Missy's kick had been powerful. The ball bounced off Willie's fingertips and into the goal cage.

Coach Harris ran to Missy and put his hand on her shoulder. "Great shot, Fremont, great shot," he called out.

Willie patted her on the back.

"Good try, Wilhelmina," said Coach Harris. "Not even an experienced goaltender could have stopped that shot. Stephanie, she faked you out. I think I can show you what she did."

Stephanie followed him, throwing Missy a backward glance. She looked mad, but Missy thought she looked just a little impressed too.

Missy put her hand into the pocket of her gym shorts. She felt the folded squares of yellow paper. They were like good-luck charms.

Missy went back to the bench and passed the notes on to Emily. When it was Emily's turn to go one-on-one, Missy figured out every time Emily was going to fake.

Missy's spirits soared. Maybe she and Emily and Wilhelmina *would* make the team. Only then would Missy be sure Baby was *really* safe after all!

CHAPTER

7

"**O**h, no, there goes another one!" cried Missy as streaks of yellow ran into the egg white in her bowl. "Hand me one more egg, Dad."

"We're out of eggs," said Mr. Fremont, peering into the refrigerator.

"How can we be out of eggs?" Missy asked.

"Easy," said Mr. Fremont. "We've used thirteen eggs trying to separate six. Let's see. I fouled up four of them. Then you took over, and we lost another three. Maybe we should take a break from breaking eggs. Your mom said that someone who's helping with the shower was planning to drop off some food here today. Let's hope eggs were on the list."

"We can't stop in the middle," said Missy. "You're already melting the chocolate. This cake takes a long time to make. Do you think I should go ahead one egg short?"

"That's *egg*sactly what I had in mind," said her father. "I don't think one egg will make a difference, especially since we've got a whole pound of chocolate."

"Okay, I'll start to beat them," said Missy. She stood on a stool, the electric beater in one hand, her stopwatch in the other. "The secret of this recipe is to whip the egg yolks for exactly five minutes."

"What happens if you do it for four minutes and forty-six seconds?" Mr. Fremont asked.

"Disaster. Everything at this party has to be perfect," said Missy. "It's for Mrs. Kaufman."

"I know how important she is to you, but perfect is not something you and I should aim for in the kitchen. Delicious, yes; perfect, no."

"Well, this time we're going to be perfect. We have to," said Missy.

The doorbell rang. "Would you get it, Missy?" said Mr. Fremont. "I have to watch the chocolate. The recipe says to take it off the heat before it is completely melted."

The doorbell rang again.

"I can't get it," replied Missy. "I'm in the middle of beating the eggs."

Her father gave her a look that meant "I'm not fooling around."

Missy turned off the beater and stopped the watch. "Remind me, Dad, I have one minute and forty-three seconds to go."

The doorbell rang for the third time.

Missy put down the beater and ran to the door, still carrying the stopwatch in her hand. When she opened it, Mrs. Kaufman was standing there, holding a large box.

"I don't think you broke any records getting to the door," joked Mrs. Kaufman, putting the box down on the hall table.

"What's this?" Missy asked.

"I'm not sure, but I know it's for the party."

"You shouldn't have to do any work. The party is for you!" exclaimed Missy.

"Oh, I didn't. Someone asked if I could stop by with these things."

"Well, thanks," said Missy. "Dad said someone was dropping off supplies for your party, but I didn't think it would be you."

"I'm happy to do it," Mrs. Kaufman replied. "It's so sweet of you and your mother to do this. I'm looking forward to the party."

"Me too," said Missy.

"Missy!" her father shouted from the kitchen. "Where are you? I need you to help whip the chocolate before it's too late."

"I've got to run," said Missy. "Thanks for bringing these by. We'll see you tomorrow."

"What are you making?" asked Mrs. Kaufman.

"It's a surprise," answered Missy. "And remember—no more lifting heavy boxes."

Mrs. Kaufman smiled. "Yes, doctor," she said. "Listen, before I go, I wanted to ask you how you're getting along with Ms. Van Sickel."

Missy tried hard not to make a face. "Well, at least I haven't flunked any more tests."

Mrs. Kaufman was shocked. "You? Flunking tests?"

"Just at the beginning," admitted Missy. "But lately things have been getting better."

"She's supposed to be an excellent teacher."

Missy sighed. "Well, anyway, we all miss you."

"I miss you too," replied Mrs. Kaufman.

"Missy!" called her father.

"I'd better go," said Missy. "Otherwise your surprise will be a disaster."

Missy said good-by to Mrs. Kaufman and carried the box into the kitchen.

"Who was that?" asked Mr. Fremont.

"Mrs. Kaufman," said Missy, looking puzzled. "She said someone asked her to drop this stuff off. Don't you think that's strange? I mean, she shouldn't have to do any work for her *own* shower."

Mr. Fremont was busy beating the chocolate with a wooden spoon. "See if she brought any eggs. I'll need to beat some into the chocolate soon."

Missy peeked into the box. "Oh, great! Eggs!" she exclaimed. She removed the carton, and she lifted out an egg. It felt light. She held it over her bowl and cracked it open. Inside was another yellow note! Missy unrolled it and read, "Don't ever slow down."

Mr. Fremont read the note over her shoulder. "That's the strangest yolk I've ever seen."

He took the note from Missy and turned it

over. " 'Don't ever slow down.' That sounds like a song."

Missy was too surprised to say anything. She took another egg out of the carton and examined it. There was a hole in the bottom of the egg, just big enough to push a rolled-up piece of paper through.

Missy cracked the other eggs open. Her father spread the notes out on the counter. Each note was numbered:

1) *Don't ever slow down.*
2) *Don't run with a frown.*
3) *When the goal is in sight—*
4) *That's no time for fright.*
5) *While playing defense—*
6) *Take out the suspense.*
7) *Like a wig on a head—*
8) *"Keep 'em covered," it said.*
9) *And speaking of heads,*
10) *Use yours and watch the point spread.*
11) *Go for it, Missy!*
12) *I know you're no sissy.*

Mr. Fremont let out a low whistle. "Somebody in the egg business certainly likes you," he said.

"The handwriting is the same as on my other notes," said Missy.

"Well, I'm very impressed," said Mr. Fremont. "Someone went to an awful lot of trouble for you. It's not easy blowing out a dozen eggs."

"Mrs. Kaufman," said Missy slowly. "Dad, it

has to be Mrs. Kaufman. I should have known. She brought the eggs over, and I thought there was a funny smile on her face."

"You mean, she was the one who sent you the book?" Mr. Fremont asked.

"It has to be her," replied Missy. "Look at lines seven and eight—they're sort of a riddle. She knows I love riddles."

Missy grinned. "I'm so happy to know who my secret coach is!" She waved a spoonful of chocolate in the air. Then she hugged her father and got chocolate all over him.

"I'm so excited!" she cried.

"I can tell," said Mr. Fremont.

"Now we *really* have to make the party perfect," said Missy. "It'll be my secret thank you to my secret coach."

Baby licked some chocolate that had fallen onto the floor. He loved chocolate.

Missy bent down and gave him a hug. "With Mrs. Kaufman as my secret coach, you're definitely safe, Baby," she said.

"I didn't know he was in danger," said Mr. Fremont.

Missy gave Baby another hug. "He was, Dad. Believe me. He was facing life with Stephanie Cook."

CHAPTER

8

On the day of the shower the doorbell rang twenty minutes before the party was supposed to begin.

"Oh, no," groaned Mrs. Fremont. She had just gotten out of the shower. "Missy, can you get that? I hate it when people come early."

Missy ran downstairs. Baby was already standing with his nose pressed against the door. Stephanie Cook and her mother stood on the doorstep.

Baby wagged his tail.

"Does he shed?" asked Mrs. Cook. She didn't even bother to greet Missy.

Missy had spent most of the morning trying to clean Baby's hair off the couch. "Just a little," she admitted. "Come on in, my mom will be down in a minute."

"Where do you want the presents?" asked

Stephanie. She was holding a gift wrapped in plaid paper with a neat green bow encircling it.

"I chose plaid because we don't know whether it's a boy or girl," said Stephanie.

"I think it's silly to use babyish wrappings, don't you?" added Mrs. Cook. "After all, Mrs. Kaufman is a grown woman. When Stephanie was born, I hated getting gifts that were too cute."

Missy put the gift on the living-room table. She tried to hide her own gift, which was wrapped in bunny-rabbit paper she had bought especially for Mrs. Kaufman's present. She had even made little bunny ears out of colored paper.

Mrs. Fremont came down the stairs, her hair still a bit damp.

"The house looks beautiful, dear," said Mrs. Cook. "I don't think I've *ever* seen it so neat."

"Thank you," said Mrs. Fremont, nearly choking. She put her arm around Missy and whispered into her ear, "Stephanie and her mother really are a perfect pair, aren't they?"

"I hope you don't mind our coming early," said Mrs. Cook. "I thought perhaps you would need help."

"How nice of you," said Mrs. Fremont, winking at Missy. "But I think we have things under control. My husband and Missy did most of the cooking. You should see the dessert—it's on display in the dining room. It was too beautiful to hide in the kitchen."

Mrs. Fremont steered Stephanie and her

mother into the dining room, where the chocolate-chocolate cake was the centerpiece of the table. It was perched high on a silver cake dish. Missy had even put yellow daisies around the plate.

"How sweet," said Mrs. Cook. "I once decorated a cake plate with flowers. Unfortunately one of the guests ate one of the flowers and became deathly ill. Perhaps I should make a sign, 'Please Don't Eat the Daisies.'" Mrs. Cook gave a little false laugh.

"I don't think we have to worry," said Mrs. Fremont. "There are plenty of other things to eat here. You'd have to be terribly hungry to eat a flower."

Missy tried hard not to laugh. Score one for her mother.

"Will you excuse me?" said Mrs. Fremont. "I do have a few last minute things to do in the kitchen."

"Oh, let me help," said Mrs. Cook.

"Really, there's nothing to do," said Mrs. Fremont.

"But I do *so* want to see what you've done with the kitchen," said Mrs. Cook. "Let me just wash my hands, and I'll be with you in a minute."

Missy showed Mrs. Cook to the bathroom. Her mother was waiting outside the kitchen door. "What a witch!" whispered Mrs. Fremont. "She almost makes me feel sorry for Stephanie. Missy, why don't you go see what Stephanie's up to. I left her alone in the dining room."

*　　*　　*

Stephanie looked up guiltily when Missy entered the room. Missy looked at the cake. There was a thumbprint on the icing.

"Uh, one of your flowers was drooping so I tried to put it back," said Stephanie.

Missy took a knife and cleaned up the frosting. "Did it taste good?" she asked.

Stephanie blushed. "I didn't taste it," she said.

"Come on, Stephanie," said Missy. "What's wrong with admitting you're human? I couldn't have been left alone in this room with that cake and not have taken a little lick."

"I did *not* lick your cake," said Stephanie. "Maybe your dog did."

"No way. Baby wouldn't take anything from the table—unless *you* gave him permission."

Missy looked down at Baby. There was a suspicious streak of chocolate around his mouth.

"But he *does* love chocolate," Missy said thoughtfully. "You didn't give him a taste, did you?"

Stephanie looked down at her feet.

Just then the doorbell rang. "I'll get it," offered Stephanie.

"Wait a minute," said Missy, following her. "This is *my* house and *my* party. *I'll* answer the door."

Missy ran to the door with Stephanie at her heels. She flung it open. A whole group of people surged into the hall, talking and laughing. The entire party had arrived at once! Mrs. Kaufman showed up with Ms. Van Sickel and three of the other teachers. Emily and Wilhelmina and their mothers stood just behind them with brightly colored packages in their hands.

Missy took Mrs. Kaufman's coat. "Thank you for the eggs," she whispered. "I know they were a lot of work."

Mrs. Kaufman laughed. "For the chickens maybe, but not for me," she said.

Missy winked at her.

"Missy?" Mrs. Kaufman said, "what—" But she was interrupted by a terrible crash from the direction of the dining room.

Missy froze. Then she ran. Ms. Van Sickel and Stephanie stood at the entrance to the dining room, staring inside.

Missy stepped between them to see what had happened. Baby's tail was between his legs. He was cowering in the corner.

Baby had gotten hold of the white tablecloth and pulled everything down around him. All the food for the party was piled on the floor! The biggest disaster was Missy's chocolate cake. It had landed upside down, and Baby had stepped in the middle of it.

Mrs. Fremont knelt beside Missy. "It's all Stephanie's fault," murmured Missy, choking back tears. "She gave Baby a taste of the frosting. Everything's ruined," Missy wailed.

"Well, we'll just have to make do with frozen pizzas," said Mrs. Fremont.

"That's not food for a baby shower," grumbled Missy.

"It's all right, Missy," said Mrs. Kaufman. "I'm gaining quite enough weight already. Besides, I love pizza."

Missy tried to smile, but she felt awful. The beautiful, perfect party was ruined. She had wanted so badly for everything to go just right. Missy had planned to take Mrs. Kaufman aside at the end of the party and thank her for being her secret coach.

Now, thanks to Stephanie, all the food was on the floor. Missy knew one thing. Today was not going to be the day she thanked Mrs. Kaufman.

Missy went into the kitchen to get the mop to clean up the mess. She stopped when she saw Ms. Van Sickel standing in front of the refrigerator. Missy had forgotten that she and her father had put the poem from the eggs on the refrigerator door.

"That's a lovely poem," said Ms. Van Sickel.

"Oh . . . thanks," stammered Missy. "It's from a special friend." She sighed. "Sorry about the cake and the big mess inside."

"I wouldn't worry about it," said Ms. Van Sickel. She studied the poem. "Unfortunately the ninth and tenth lines of the poem don't scan. The poet could have done a better job of working them out rhythmically."

Missy rolled her eyes. "I think it's perfect just the way it is," she insisted.

Ms. Van Sickel shrugged and returned to the party.

Missy stared at the notes. Tears filled her eyes. The poem *was* perfect. If only the party had been perfect too.

CHAPTER 9

The day after the party Missy woke up early. She stared at the ceiling. Even Baby's warm breath next to her was no comfort. If only Stephanie hadn't ruined everything. It was true that the party had not been a total disaster. Mrs. Kaufman seemed to enjoy opening presents between bites of pizza, but there was nothing *special* about the party. Nothing to let Mrs. Kaufman know that she, Missy, loved her for being her secret coach.

Missy got out of bed and went to her desk. She opened the special box made out of Italian marble that her grandmother had brought her from Europe. This was the box in which Missy kept her most valuable possessions. On the bottom were Baby's papers declaring that he was a purebred Old English sheepdog. On the top lay the yellow notes from Missy's secret coach.

"I have to get the courage to thank Mrs. Kaufman," Missy said out loud. She looked at Baby. "The sooner the better."

Baby cocked his head at her.

Missy looked out the window. It was a beautiful, sunny fall day. She remembered the first day of her shape-up routine, before she had a secret coach. That very first day she had run into Mrs. Kaufman. Perhaps that was when Mrs. Kaufman decided to be her secret coach.

Missy put Baby on his leash. They walked to Mrs. Kaufman's house. Missy looked at her watch. It was still only seven o'clock—much too early to ring the doorbell. But maybe Mrs. Kaufman would be leaving soon to walk Cleo.

Missy paced back and forth in front of the Kaufmans' house. The red front door remained firmly shut. The sun was shining directly into the windows, so Missy couldn't see if anyone was moving around inside.

Missy and Baby made their twenty-fourth pass in front of the house, when the red door finally opened.

Mrs. Kaufman came outside, followed by Cleo. Cleo ran over to Baby, wagging her tail.

"Missy, what are you doing here?" Mrs. Kaufman asked.

"Oh, I just happened to be walking by," said Missy.

Mrs. Kaufman laughed. "Missy, my husband

said that a girl and her dog, the size of a small bear, were on patrol all morning. He's been watching you pace up and down in front of the house. Why didn't you ring the doorbell? I wanted to thank you for the party yesterday."

"I didn't want to wake you," said Missy.

Mrs. Kaufman shook her head. "Come inside for a minute. I want to introduce you to my husband."

Missy stepped inside and looked around curiously. The walls of the living room were painted a light pink and the furniture was all white. Missy thought it was the prettiest house she had ever seen.

Mr. Kaufman came out of the kitchen carrying a cup of coffee. He had short curly red hair and a long narrow face. He smiled at Missy. "Is this the young lady who's been guarding our house?" he asked.

"This is Missy Fremont," Mrs. Kaufman replied, "and her dog, Baby. I've told you about Missy."

Missy swallowed hard. Mrs. Kaufman had been talking about her to her husband! Missy wondered if he knew about the notes. Maybe he had helped her blow out the eggs and stick in the notes. It must have been a hard job, the kind of work that would be easier done by two people. Mr. Kaufman was looking at Missy with just the faintest hint of a twinkle in his eye, as if he and Missy shared a secret.

Missy took a deep breath. "Mrs. Kaufman, I

came this morning to thank you," she said formally.

"Thank *me*?" exclaimed Mrs. Kaufman. "It's *I* who have to thank *you* for the wonderful party. Someday I've got to try that chocolate cake that Baby liked so much."

"Well, it needs real eggs," said Missy. "Your ingredients make great poetry, but they're not very good for a cake."

Mr. and Mrs. Kaufman looked at Missy as if she were speaking another language. "What are you talking about?" asked Mr. Kaufman carefully.

"Didn't you help Mrs. Kaufman with the eggs?" Missy asked.

Mrs. Kaufman laughed a little nervously. "Was something wrong with the eggs, Missy? Because I didn't even buy them. I found the box on my doorstep. A note on it said that it was needed for the party and asked if I could drop it off at your house. If the eggs were rotten, I'm sorry, but it wasn't my fault."

"Nothing was wrong with them," insisted Missy. "I thought it was so cute—you know, what you had done."

"Missy, I don't understand," said Mrs. Kaufman.

"The poem you put in the eggs, and all the notes you sent me."

"What notes?"

Missy took out the notes that she had carefully saved. "Didn't you send me these?" she asked.

Mrs. Kaufman studied the notes. She showed

them to her husband. "I've never seen them, honestly. How did you get them?"

Missy studied Mrs. Kaufman's face. She certainly looked as if she were telling the truth.

"The first one was tucked into Baby's collar," explained Missy. She told Mrs. Kaufman and her husband all about the book and the secret notes of encouragement.

"It certainly wasn't me. I wish it was," said Mrs. Kaufman. "But it wasn't."

Missy believed her. But if it wasn't Mrs. Kaufman, who *was* it?

CHAPTER 10

Missy jumped up and down on the edge of the soccer field, trying to stay loose. Her mother had brought Baby to the field to watch the tryouts for the soccer team. Missy was so nervous she could hardly think.

Stephanie stood down the line from her. The coach had divided them into two teams. Stephanie, Missy, and Emily had ended up on the same line. Wilhelmina was playing goalie.

Missy wondered what Stephanie would do to try to make her look bad. She would probably hog the ball the whole time.

"Don't be nervous," said Mrs. Fremont. "Just think of all the work you've put in. Do your best."

Missy hated it when people told her not to be

nervous. How could she not be nervous? Her dog's entire future might be at stake.

The coach blew his whistle. Missy ran out to midfield. As they started down the field, Stephanie tried to drive the ball too fast and lost control of it. The other team got the ball and scored a goal.

Missy thought Stephanie might as well have been playing by herself.

"Use your head out there," called Coach Harris. "Cook, you've got two good players on either side of you."

The next time Stephanie got the ball, she tried to drive it past her defender and lost it again. The defender passed the ball up to the wing, and they scored a second time.

"You're doing great, Stephanie," muttered Missy. "What happens to our bet if *none* of us makes the team?"

Stephanie threw her a dirty look.

"Come on," said Missy. "The coach is looking for *team* players, not just good players."

"Missy's right," said Emily. "The way you're playing, we all lose."

Stephanie didn't answer. But the next time someone was about to take the ball, she passed it neatly to Missy. Missy was so surprised that she almost lost it. Then she remembered the yellow notes. "Short choppy steps," Missy repeated to herself. She dribbled down the field, keeping the ball in control. Just as she was about to lose the ball, she passed it to Emily. Emily kicked it high into the air.

Willie jumped up, but the ball was over her head.

A goal by Emily! Missy hugged her. Then she glanced at Stephanie. "Good pass, Stephanie," said Missy.

Stephanie didn't smile. But she didn't crack any jokes about Baby either.

The next time Missy got the ball, she passed it to Stephanie. Stephanie hesitated a fraction of a second. Then she kicked the ball toward the goal—but not hard enough. Wilhelmina fielded the ball easily.

Five minutes later they were near the goal again. Stephanie passed the ball to Missy. Missy wrapped her foot around the ball. The ball curved in midair, hit the top of the goal post, and bounced in. Willie dove for it, but she didn't have a chance.

As they were running up the field, Stephanie nodded at Missy. "Good kick," she said.

But Missy looked at her suspiciously.

"What are you up to?" she asked. "That's the second good pass you've given me."

Stephanie said nothing.

Coach Harris blew his whistle and called the players into the center. "You've got a natural rhythm together," he told Stephanie, Emily, and Missy. "I want you three on my team. And Wilhelmina. She's shaping up as a good goaltender.

But I want the three of you to be on the same line."

"Stephanie and me together," groaned Missy. "What a disaster!"

"Maybe yes, maybe no," said Stephanie as she watched Coach Harris go to the sideline for his clipboard.

"What does that mean?" asked Missy.

"I watched the way you three shaped up for soccer," said Stephanie. "I knew you'd make the team. I guess I don't mind being on the same side—at least on the playing field."

"Does this mean we're friends?" asked Missy.

"Please," Stephanie said with a groan. "Let's not push it! But you can relax about your big Baby. He's safe now."

"Thanks a lot," said Missy. But she shook her head. She had a feeling she would never understand Stephanie Cook.

Missy saw her mother waving to her. She ran to the sidelines and told her that she had made the team.

"Congratulations!" cried Mrs. Fremont.

"I owe most of it to my secret coach," said Missy. "But I still don't know who that is."

Coach Harris joined the Fremonts. "I guess you've heard the good news," he said to Mrs. Fremont.

"Missy just told me. You couldn't get a harder worker."

"Well, she's certainly improved," said Coach

Harris. "Say, isn't that Hortense Van Sickel over there?" Coach Harris pointed to Ms. Van Sickel, who was standing by herself on the sidelines.

"Yes, she's Missy's new teacher. She's taken over Mrs. Kaufman's class."

"I *thought* I recognized her," Coach Harris said. "She was once an all-star collegiate soccer player—and a great one too."

"Ms. Van Sickel!" Missy exclaimed.

Coach Harris nodded. "She's one of the best. What she doesn't know about soccer hasn't been invented."

Missy looked toward the sidelines at her teacher. Slowly, the pieces of the puzzle began to fall into place—the poem on the refrigerator, Ms. Van Sickel's presence at soccer practice. Yes, it all made perfect sense. Missy bit her lip and thought for a minute. Then she nodded. She knew just what to do.

"Excuse me," said Missy. "There's something I've got to take care of."

Missy found her notebook and tore out a piece of paper. "Thanks for being such a good coach," she wrote. Then she slipped the note under Baby's collar.

She pointed Baby in Ms. Van Sickel's direction and gave him a little push. Baby trotted over to her and nudged Ms. Van Sickel's skirt. The teacher bent down, read the note, and smiled.

A few minutes later Baby returned with a new note—and the answer to the mystery—on his collar. "You're welcome, Missy. You were a great student."